STAR

OF

WONDER

LEENA LANE AND ELENA BABONI

Contents

Set in a small occupied country, more than two thousand years ago, this is the story of the birth of Mary's son, from the visit of the angel Gabriel to the flight of the holy family to Egypt, and their return after the death of King Herod. *Star of Wonder* is the story of the first Christmas, a celebration of the birth of Jesus, Son of God, King of kings, Prince of Peace.

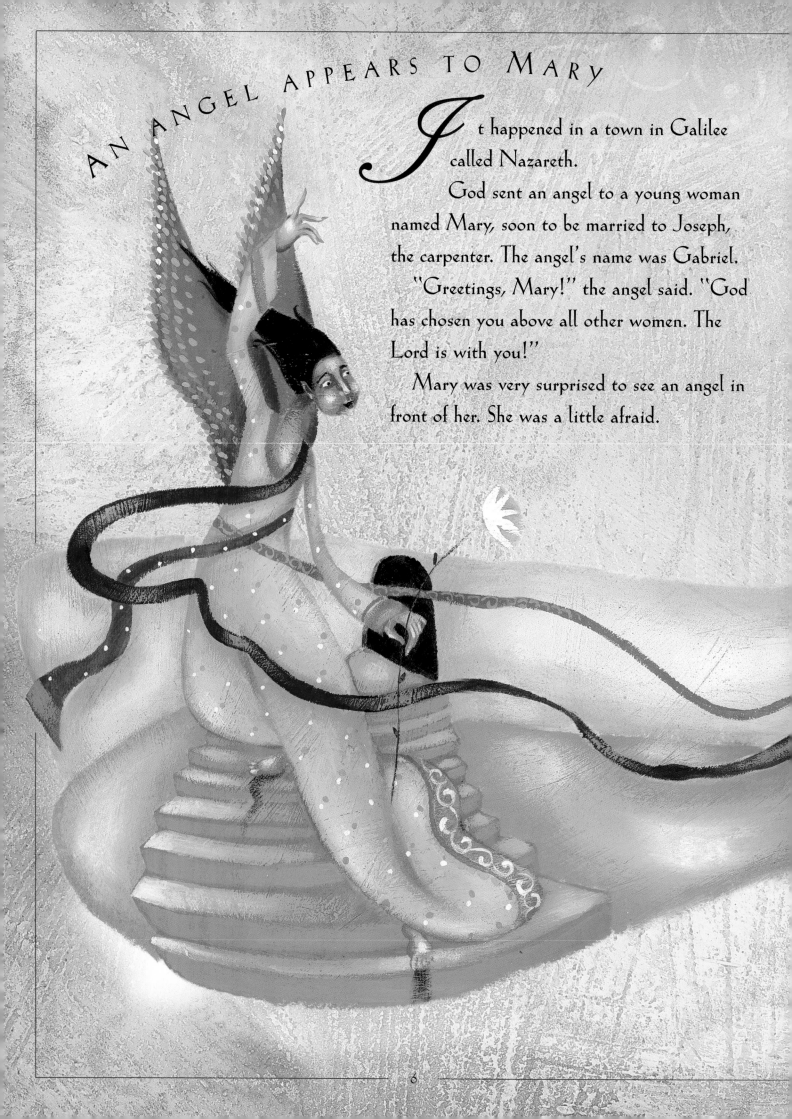

*I*t happened in a town in Galilee called Nazareth.

God sent an angel to a young woman named Mary, soon to be married to Joseph, the carpenter. The angel's name was Gabriel.

"Greetings, Mary!" the angel said. "God has chosen you above all other women. The Lord is with you!"

Mary was very surprised to see an angel in front of her. She was a little afraid.

"Don't be afraid, Mary," continued the angel. "God is pleased with you. You are going to have a baby boy. You will call him Jesus. He will be the Son of the Most High God. His kingdom will never end."

"But… but how can this be?" asked Mary. "I'm not even married yet."

"The Holy Spirit will come to you and your child will be called God's own son," replied the angel. "Nothing is impossible with God."

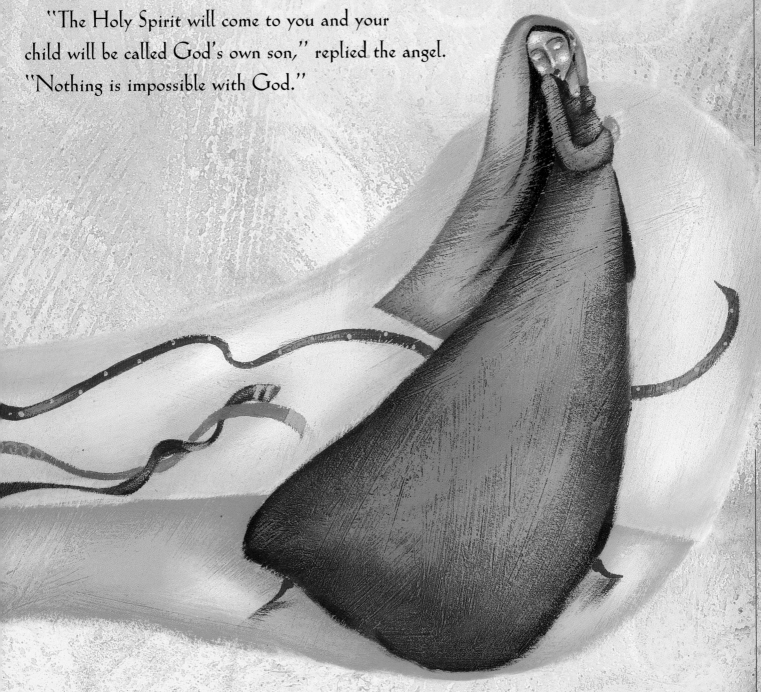

"I am the Lord's servant," said Mary, bowing her head. "Let all these things happen just as you have said."

The angel returned to heaven; and Mary praised God with all her heart.

Caesar Augustus, the mighty Roman Emperor, wanted to count all the people who lived in the Roman Empire. Every man was ordered to travel back to the town his family came from.

For Mary's husband, Joseph, this meant a long journey on foot to the town of Bethlehem.

But it was also a very long journey for Mary. A donkey carried their bundles and water jars, but Mary had to carry a heavy load too:

the baby in her womb would soon be ready to be born.

The road was stony and dusty. Mary stumbled from time to time; she often became breathless. Joseph helped her along and they rested wherever they found a shady olive tree.

"Are we nearly there?" asked Mary hopefully.

At last they could see the lights of Bethlehem in the distance. At last they had reached their journey's end.

Joseph knocked on the door of the first inn they reached when they came to Bethlehem.

"Do you have a room for a few nights?" Joseph asked the innkeeper. "My wife needs to rest. She is going to have a baby soon."

"Sorry," came the reply. "We're fully booked." And the door was closed.

Joseph turned to Mary. She looked tired and pale. They had to find somewhere for her to lie down.

"We'll try another inn," said Joseph. And he knocked on the door of the inn further down the road. But it was the same story. No room.

"What shall we do now?" asked Mary.

Joseph shook his head. He didn't know what to do.

Just then, another innkeeper peered out of a doorway.

"I don't have any rooms in the inn," he said, "but I can see that your wife must rest somewhere. I can let you stay in the barn behind the house. My animals are there, but the straw is clean. I can bring you some food and water."

"Thank you," said Joseph. "You are very kind."

The innkeeper led Mary and Joseph behind the house. Cows and donkeys were resting on the straw. Mary sat down to rest and closed her eyes. She felt very tired. But she was thankful for the innkeeper's kindness to them. She knew that her baby was going to be born soon.

NO ROOM AT THE INN

The night was quiet. There was the sound of the cicadas outside and the snuffling of the calves in the straw inside. The wind was blowing and the door creaked.

Mary tried to rest. This was not how she had imagined it, the birth of her first-born child. She thought she would be at home, with her mother and neighbors to help her. She thought she would be lying on her own bed in Nazareth. But she was here, in the straw in Bethlehem, surrounded by animals and with no one but Joseph to help. Then Mary remembered the words of the angel Gabriel: "Do not be afraid, Mary…"

A BABY IN THE MANGER

The cry of an infant broke the stillness of the night. Mary cradled her baby in her arms.

"His name is Jesus," panted Mary, exhausted but filled with wonderful joy.

Joseph looked at the helpless baby in Mary's arms. He knew that this was a very special child.

Mary tenderly wrapped the tiny baby in clean cloths, held him close, then put him in a manger to sleep.

On the hills near Bethlehem, the sky was filled with dazzling light. God had sent an angel to bring good news for all the world!

"Do not be afraid!" the angel said. "I bring good news of great joy! Today in Bethlehem a Savior has been born: he is Christ the Lord. And so that you know that this is true, you will find a baby wrapped in cloths and lying in a manger."

The shepherds on the hillside were speechless. What could this mean? An angel, here, visiting them with their sheep?

Suddenly a huge choir of angels appeared, praising God in
beautiful voices and saying:

"Glory to God in the highest, and on earth, peace."

The shepherds had never seen such a wonderful
sight; they had not heard such a beautiful
sound. It was the music of heaven.

GOOD NEWS OF GREAT JOY

The shepherds looked at one another in amazement.

"Did you see that?" said one of the men.

"Quick!" said a young shepherd. "We must hurry to Bethlehem and see this great thing which has happened. God has told us about it — we must see it for ourselves!"

So the shepherds left their sheep and ran all the way down the hill to the town.

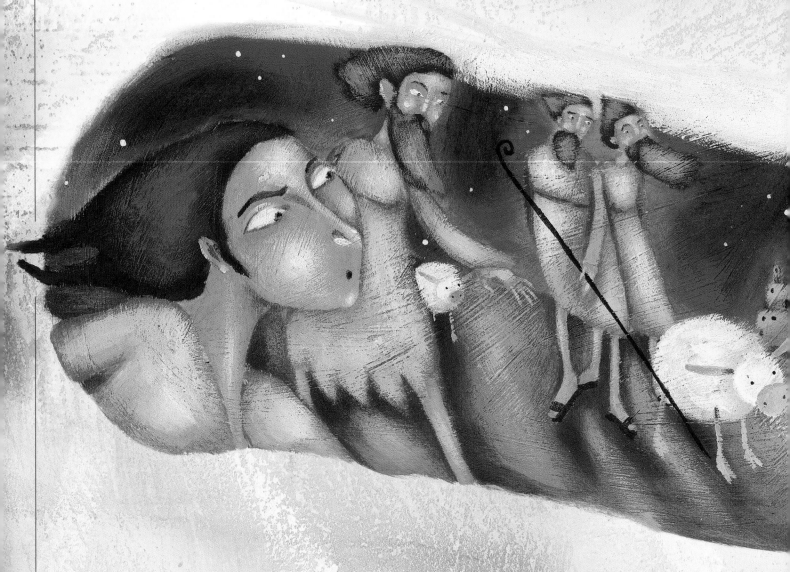

They looked up and down the quiet streets. Nothing stirred.

Then they heard the faint sound of a tiny baby crying. The shepherds followed the sounds to the place behind the inn. They saw the animals resting. They saw Mary, bending over the manger, stroking her baby's little face.

"This must be the baby the angels spoke of," said the shepherds.

"This is the one born to be our Savior!"

Mary looked puzzled. The young shepherd quickly explained to Mary how the angels had come to tell them the good news.

SHEPHERDS FIND THE BABY

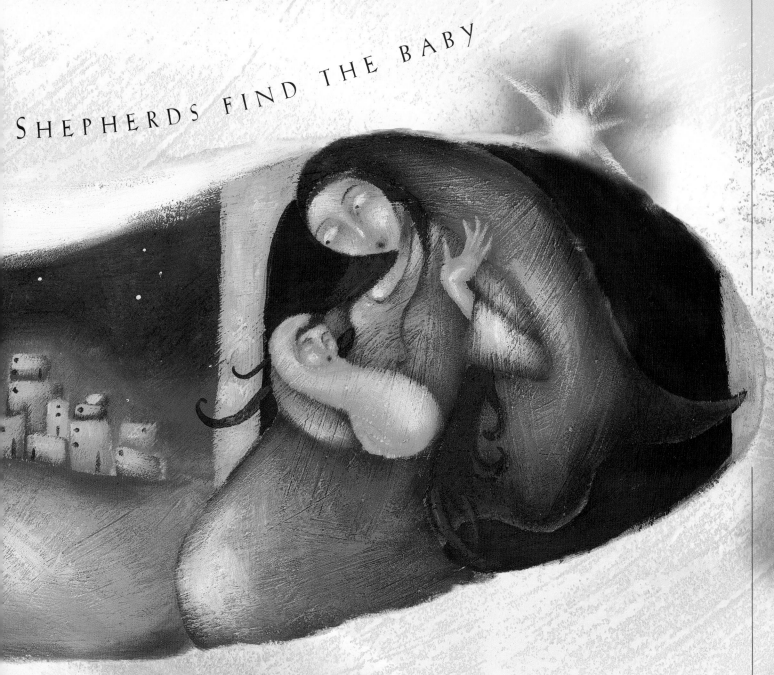

And while he spoke, Mary's eyes filled with tears. She knew she would always treasure their words in her heart.

The shepherds returned to their flocks, praising God for all that they had seen and heard.

It was all just as the angel had told them.

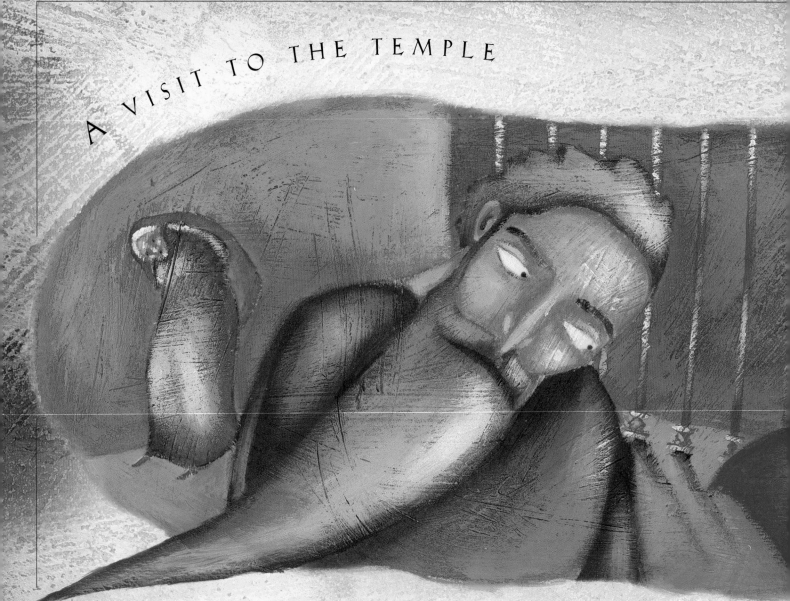

When Jesus was about a month old, Mary and Joseph took him to the Temple in Jerusalem. It was a very special day for them all. As was the custom for all baby boys at that time, Jesus was going to be presented to God in the Temple.

Mary and Joseph took with them two young doves to offer as a sacrifice. They wanted to thank God for the birth of Jesus and to ask God to bless him.

A very old man called Simeon was waiting at the Temple. He had prayed to God all his life and believed that one day the Savior would come.

Simeon saw Mary and Joseph carrying Jesus into the Temple courts. He knew at once that this was a very special child. Simeon took Jesus in his arms and praised God:

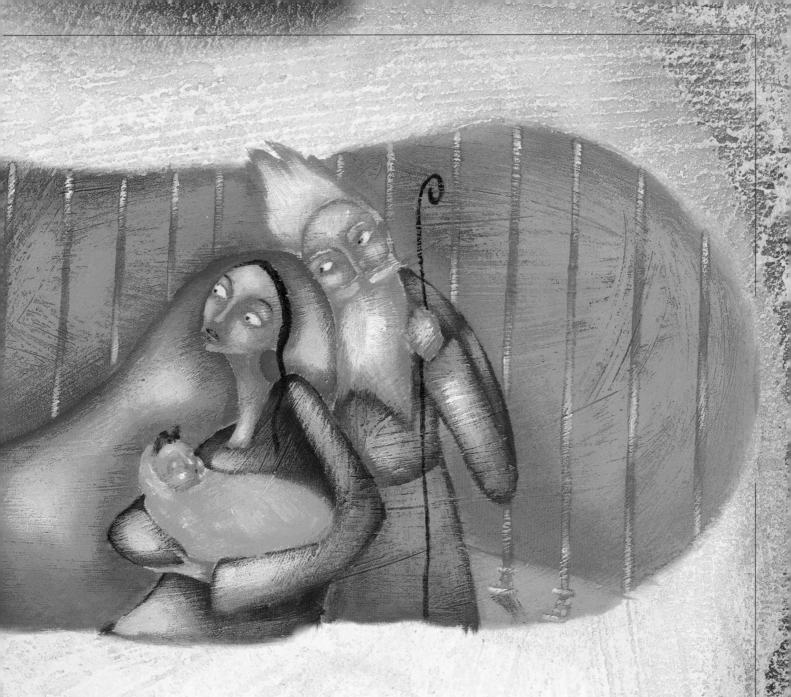

"Lord of all, I can now go peacefully from this life. For my eyes have seen the Savior, who brings light to all people on earth!"

There was also a very old lady in the Temple that day. She was a prophetess called Anna. She worshiped there day and night.

Anna came up to Mary and Joseph and looked with wonder at the baby Jesus. She gave thanks to God for the special child in his mother's arms. Anna knew that this was the baby God had promised God's people.

There were wise men in the east who tracked the course of stars and constellations in the sky. They knew the position and time at which stars would appear.

One clear night, they were gazing at the jeweled sky above: bright stars, dim stars far away, planets, shooting stars, asteroids, and galaxies beyond.

Suddenly, one of the wise men spoke.

"Look at that!" he said, pointing with excitement at the sky. "Surely that is a new star! It's so much brighter than all the others!"

WISE MEN FROM THE EAST

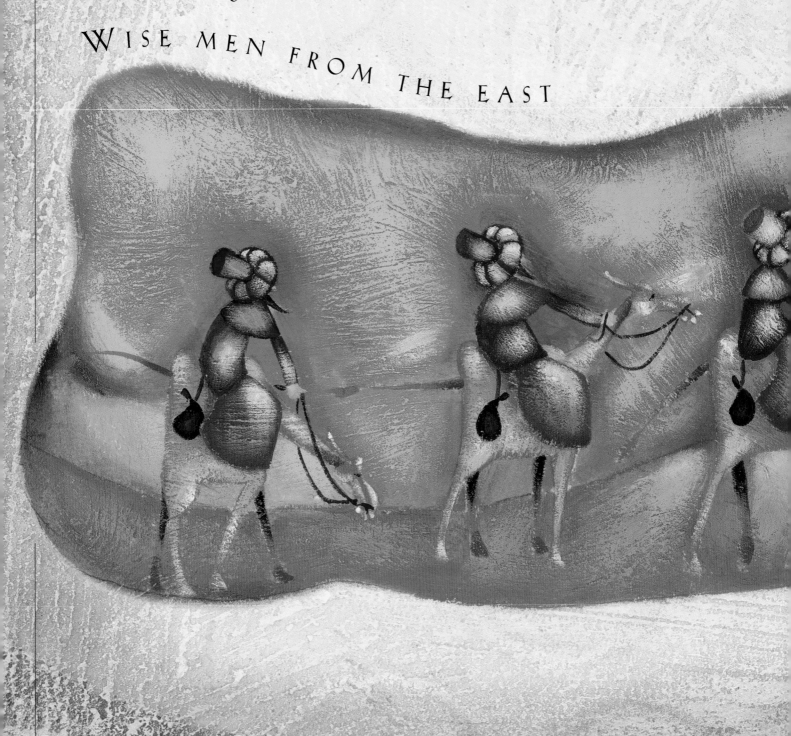

"You're right!" said the other wise men. "It is indeed a new star!"

"What can it mean?" they asked each other.

"Something magnificent has happened in the world!" said the first wise man. "It is a sign that a new king has been born, the child who will be King of the Jews."

"Then we must go and find this king!" said the others. "We will follow his star!"

The wise men loaded their camels and set off across the desert, bearing gifts. The star guided them westward to Judea, to the great city of Jerusalem.

King Herod the Great ruled over Judea.

He was a cruel man.

Riches and power were the only important things in his life.

If anyone got in his way, Herod would crush them.

The wise men arrived at Herod's palace. They did not know that Herod was a wicked man. The star had seemed to guide them to this place. After all, a palace was the place where a new king might be born.

"Where is the new king?" asked the wise men. "We saw his star in the sky and have come to worship him!"

Herod barely controlled his rising anger. What were these men talking about?

There was room for only one king here! He called together the priests and teachers of the law.

"Where is the child who has been born king?" asked Herod.

"It says in the Scriptures that he will be born in Bethlehem, your Majesty," said the priests.

Herod thought hard about what to do. He must get rid of this new king. He alone, Herod the Great, would be king in this land! He hatched a plot.

"Go to Bethlehem!" said Herod to the wise men. "When you have found the child, come back and tell me, so that I, too, may go and worship him."

So the wise men set off again toward the little town of Bethlehem.

The star guided the wise men onward. It seemed to rest above a house in Bethlehem. There was no palace to be seen, only some shabby-looking houses with flat roofs. Chickens squawked through the streets, children ran after each other, and clothes were drying in the sun.

"I feel sure that this is the right house!" said one of the wise men, pointing to a dwelling in front of them.

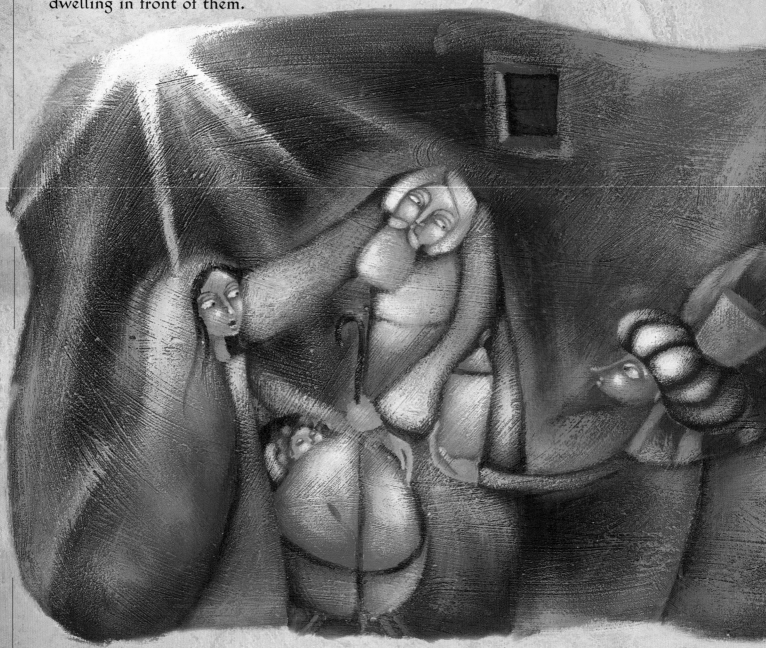

The wise men went quietly inside. They saw Mary, holding a young child in her arms. 'We have come to worship the new king!' said the first man. "We have traveled far."

Then they all bowed down low and worshiped Jesus. They opened their bags and brought out beautiful gifts from the east: gold, frankincense, and myrrh. These were royal gifts, gifts for a king.

Mary thanked the wise men and treasured their gifts. She could not fully understand what they said to her, but she knew why they had come. Jesus was born to be king.

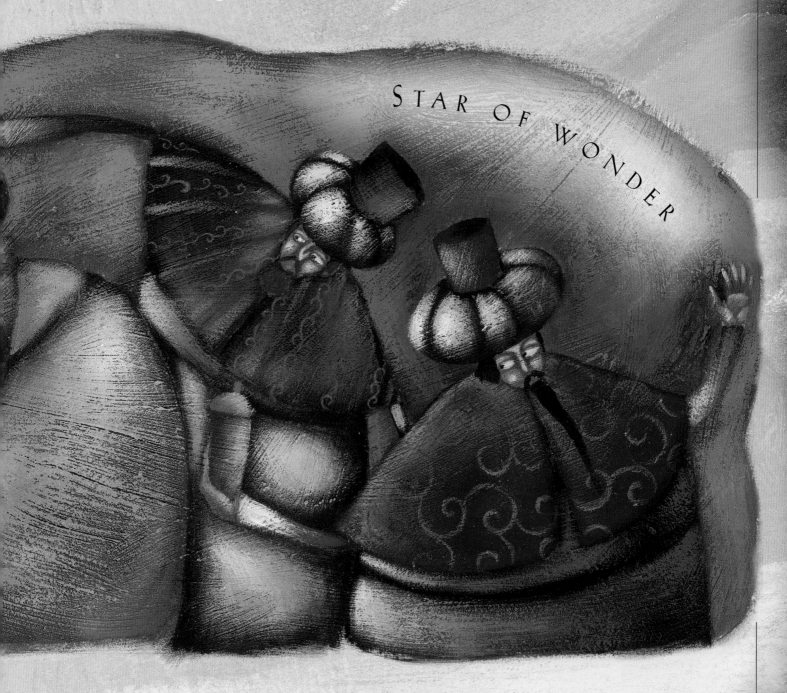

STAR OF WONDER

The wise men were warned by God in a dream not to return to Herod's palace. So they set off back to their homelands in the east, marveling at what they had seen.

When the wise men had left, Mary and Joseph settled down for the night.

But that night, Joseph had a terrible dream. He called out to Mary.

"What's the matter?" asked Mary sleepily.

"We must go from here at once! An angel appeared to me in my dreams. He said I must take the child and his mother and escape to Egypt. Mary, we must go. And we must stay away until God tells us it is safe to return. Herod wants to find Jesus and kill him!"

Mary was very afraid. At once she packed their things together and gently lifted Jesus.

"If God has warned us in this way, then we must go," she said. "There's not a moment to lose!"

It was not yet daylight, but Joseph and Mary crept out into the dark streets of

THE FLIGHT INTO EGYPT

Bethlehem and set off along the road leading out of the town. They hoped no one had seen them leave.

"It's a long way to Egypt, Mary," said Joseph.

"I know," replied Mary, holding Jesus tightly. "But God will look after us. God won't let any harm come to Jesus. God has a plan for him."

Some time later, Herod's soldiers searched all the houses in Bethlehem, trying to find Jesus. But they were too late. God's angel had guided Joseph, Mary, and Jesus to safety.

Years passed and King Herod the Great died. His son, Archelaus, became King of Judea.

Mary, Joseph, and Jesus were still living in Egypt. Then, one night, the angel of the Lord appeared to Joseph in another dream.

"Joseph," said the angel. "It is safe to return to Israel. The people who were trying to kill Jesus are now dead."

When Joseph awoke, he told Mary what the angel had said.

"It is time to go home," Mary told her little son.

At last the time had come to return to their homeland, where their families and friends lived. Mary was looking forward to showing everyone her special son.

Joseph, Mary, and Jesus traveled for many days until they reached Galilee. Over the brow of a hill they saw the little town of Nazareth. Mary's heart leapt for joy. At last they could make a real home for their family.

Jesus grew up in Nazareth, strong and wise. And God was with him.

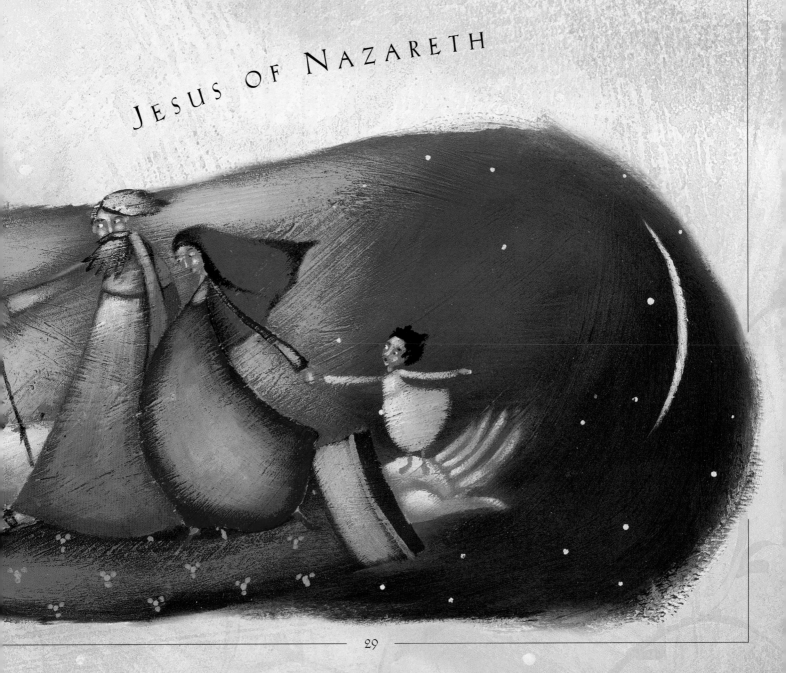

JESUS OF NAZARETH

Published in the United States of America by
Abingdon Press, 201 Eighth Avenue South, Nashville, Tennessee 37202
ISBN 978-0-687-64391-2

First edition 2007

Copyright © 2007 Anno Domini Publishing
1 Churchgates, The Wilderness, Berkhamsted, Herts HP4 2UB
Text copyright © 2007 AD Publishing Ltd, Leena Lane
Illustrations copyright © 2007 Elena Baboni

Publishing Director Annette Reynolds
Editor Nicola Bull
Art Director Gerald Rogers
Pre-production Krystyna Kowalska Hewitt
Production John Laister

Bible stories can be found as follows:
An angel appears to Mary, Luke 1:26-38
The journey to Bethlehem, Luke 2:1-5
No room at the inn, Luke 2:6-7
A baby in the manger, Luke 2:7
Good news of great joy, Luke 2:8-14
Shepherds find the baby, Luke 2:15-20
A visit to the temple, Luke 2:21-38
Wise men from the east, Matthew 2:1-2
The king in the palace, Matthew 2:3-8
Star of wonder, Matthew 2:9-12
The flight into Egypt, Matthew 2:13-15
Jesus of Nazareth, Matthew 2:19-23; Luke 2:39-40

Printed and bound in Singapore

11/07
14.00